Nerdi Bunny

and the

Forever Family Safari

by

Aisha Toombs

First Printing, 2020

ISBN: 978-1-7337947-5-6

For "Neeve" and the loving family I was given;
and the unconditional family I chose.

Dear Reader:

Be your BEST self and LIVE your BEST life.

NEVER let the darkness of the world POACH your
spirit.

Standing up for the good of ALL is ALWAYS worth it.

LOVE is Love.

Hugs,

A.T.

Contents

Farewell, My Friend 1

Ollie and Ellie 7

Welcome to the Sanctuary......................... 11

Stumped for Solutions 16

Rhino Problems, Mane Events................. 21

Pride. Stalk. Prowl 28

Last Stop, Buffalo.. 33

No Bunny is 100 Percent 37

Showdown at the Falls................................. 41

Forever Family... 47

Farewell My Friend

It was the last day of school and time to say farewell to Ashura, an exchange student in Nerdi's class visiting from Africa. Ashura spent the year in Cottontail Burrow while Hamilton Shanks was chosen to spend the year at Ashura's school in the Savanna. Before dismissing for the summer, all the students in Nerdi's class gathered to celebrate in the school yard for a big farewell celebration of drumming, dancing, food, and well-wishes. Of all the end of the year celebrations, this one was bittersweet as Nerdi and Ashura became quite close, bonding over their shared love of books.

"Before you go, Ashura—I wanted to give you this," Nerdi said as she handed Ashura a box wrapped in golden paper and matching curly ribbon.

"What's this? You didn't have to get me anything, Nerdi," Ashura responded as he took the box shaking his head.

"I know, but you're going to have a long flight back to the Savanna so...," as Nerdi trailed off, Ashura looked down at the box and neatly began ripping off the paper.

"Nerdi!! Is this the next book in the Mew and Squeak chronicles? Thank you so much!"

"You're very welcome, Ashura. I know how much

you liked them. I was surprised since the first one was a romance."

"What--boys can't enjoy romance novels? It is romance, but it is full of adventure and intrigue! I'm very excited to read the next one and also excited to have some of your mother's muffins and buttery jam." Ashura took his friend by the paw and walked over to the refreshment table. Ashura got Nerdi a cup of juice and a muffin for himself.

"Do you have any plans for the summer, Nerdi?" Ashura asked as he took a bite of his muffin with buttery jam.

"No," Nerdi replied, "not this time. I was hoping to catch up on some reading and relax this summer. How about you?"

"The same. But I am going to miss Cottontail Burrow and your mama's muffins and jam. These are magnificent!"

"Is that all, Ashura?" Nerdi asked with her whiskers in a frown-like smile.

"And you, of course, Nerdi," Ashura laughed.

"Aww, I'm going to miss you too, Ashura." Nerdi chuckled and poked her friend, making him laugh. Nerdi was also going to miss the sound of Ashura's voice. She loved his accent; it reminded Nerdi of sunsets. She always looked forward to hearing him read during class.

"I spoke to Hamilton yesterday and he is eager to return home. He misses you and his family very much. I have to admit, I miss mine as well. But we will write and call each other once in a while, yes?"

"Definitely."

"And you will maybe come visit someday?" asked Ashura.

"I would LOVE that!" Nerdi hugged Ashura one more time, promising to keep in touch.

***

The first few weeks of summer were perfect and filled with lazy days. Everything was quiet in the Bunny house since Artsy and Sporty left for camp. Hamilton returned home for a few days, but soon hit the road with his parents to spend his summer with them while they were on a fitness tour. Nerdi was looking forward to her first call with Ashura since his return to the Savanna.

In the meantime, she had been reading all about the lion, rhino and elephant populations that lived there and couldn't wait to ask Ashura questions. Calling back and forth from the Savanna to Cottontail Burrow was quite expensive, so Nerdi took on extra chores around the house. She spent afternoons weeding the garden and cleaning the kitchen, and with the extra allowance, paid for their phone calls.

Nerdi wrapped her ears around her face. She got so caught up in her reading that she forgot to clean the kitchen. "Mama," Nerdi mumbled from under her puffs, "it's almost time for my call with Ashura.

Is it okay if I clean the kitchen afterwards?" she asked.

"Did you lose track of time again, Nerdine?"

"I did. I'm sorry, Mama. I was reading all about the elephants and I wanted to ask Ashura about some of his friends."

Mama tilted her head to the side and said, "Tell you what—go start on the kitchen until your call comes through and then you can finish cleaning the rest of the kitchen after your call."

Nerdi hopped to the kitchen and put on her cleaning apron. Looking around, she wasn't quite sure where to start.

"Maybe I should begin with my least favorite thing— scrubbing the floors," Nerdi mumbled. But then she remembered that she also needed to wipe down the cupboards and dust. The dust was only going to end up on her clean floor and that meant she'd have to clean the floors twice! Nerdi put on her earphones, cranked up her music, and got to work.

It had only been a few minutes before Mama tapped Nerdi on the shoulder as she was wiping down the cupboards. Mama's face was soft and serious, holding the phone. Nerdi removed her earphones. "What's wrong, Mama?"

"It's Ashura…" Mama's whiskers turned down into a heavy frown and Nerdi's mind went a few different places, but hopeful that her friend was okay. She took the phone from Mama.

"Hello?"

"Hello, Nerdi," Ashura said with a blend of happiness and heaviness. "It is good to hear your voice."

"You too…but…what's the matter?" Nerdi asked.

"I'm sorry it has taken so long for me to call, but when I returned it was to some terrible news. My friends that I told you about, Ollie and Ellie? Well, they have been separated from their herd. The whole sanctuary has been trying to find them, but we have not been successful. I know you were trying to relax this summer, but we could use your help."

Nerdi turned around to look at Mama. She was holding up two suitcases with a small warm smile. Nerdi then said to her friend, "We'll see you in about a day or two."

Ollie and Ellie

The moon's reflection cast on the watering hole like a huge pearl illuminating the entire camp. Ollie and Ellie loved nights like this one with their mama, Tussie. She would gather them around the cool pools of water and share stories from when she was a young elephant. The rest of the herd was sound asleep except for Aunt Izzie, who was keeping watch for trouble.

"Mama," Ollie began, "will I grow tusks like yours?"

"Maybe, Ollie. But it takes a long time. It doesn't happen overnight. Your aunt is still growing hers."

Tussie's tusks were long and pearly and almost touched the ground. If you looked at her face-on, her tusks looked like they formed a heart shape.

"Mama?" Ollie began again, "are there other herds out there, like ours?"

Ollie's sister Ellie answered, "Ollie, of course there are other herds out there."

"Well, I never see them," Ollie retorted, "Our family is the only family I know."

"Yes, Ollie," Tussie started, "There are other herds out there, some with more elephants, others with less. Some come and go. You're too young to remember, but everyone in our herd wasn't always with us. I didn't start here."

"What do you mean, Mama?" asked Ollie.

"Well, remember the place we visit—the Sanctuary?"

Ollie nodded, "Yes, where Ashura lives."

"Yes. Your aunt and I were raised there with other elephants and when we were old enough to head out on our own, Bibi took us into her herd."

"Tell us about, Bibi, Mama." Ellie asked, "Was she nice?"

"Bibi was strong and kind and generous. She did not have any daughters of her own, but she treated Izzie and I like we were her own; teaching us everything we needed to know in order to take care of our own herd someday."

Ollie leaned into Mama, taking in her warmth before saying, "And now this is your herd, Mama."

Tussie nodded and held her boy close. She then turned and smoothed the ears of her daughter, Ellie. "Bibi would always say: 'Every elephant needs a herd'. She taught us how to take care of the herd because she wouldn't always be here."

"One day Ellie will lead the herd or join another, right?"

Tussie laughed softly, "If she wants to, Ollie."

"Not for a long time, Ollie" his sister answered.

"Mama still has a lot to teach me."

Suddenly, Aunt Izzie began to rumble softly, stirring and waking the members of the herd that were sleeping soundly or resting.

"What's going on Mama," Ollie asked. Tussie motioned for them to follow her and rejoin the herd. As they made their way to the group, she noticed several figures spreading out in the brush surrounding her and her children. Tussie made eye contact with her sister Izzie and then let out a roaring trumpet, causing most of the herd to stampede. Aunt Izzie and two other elephants remained, trying to mob the figures surrounding Tussie, Ollie and Ellie.

"What do we do, Mama?!" cried Ollie. Ellie looked behind her brother and, although she couldn't see them, she could hear the figures getting closer.

"Those tusks are amazing," snarled a voice in the darkness, "Some of the best I've ever seen. And I should know because no one knows more about tusks than me." Aunt Izzie and the other elephants were distracting the other intruders, but Ellie could now see the figure with his long snout and tiny claws getting closer to her, Mama, and Ollie. Tussie could see it too and looked down at her children.

"No matter what happens," Tussie whispered, "—no matter what you hear—you two keep running, do you understand? Do you remember the way—where I took you—do you remember the tree—where I told you to go if we got separated?"

"Yes, Mama," Ollie and Ellie said as they unknotted

their trunks from around her.

"But what about you--" Ellie didn't get to finish.

"Now run!" Mama yelled. Ollie and Ellie stamped off as fast as they could, away from the water and the pearly moon towards the blurry horizon. As they ran, they could hear their mother's mighty trumpet in the distance...

Crack!
Crack!

Boom!

Silence.

Ellie woke up each night hoping it was all just a bad dream. Each night Ollie curled up beside her, often whimpering and crying in his sleep. When Mama didn't come to calm him down, Ellie knew that the bad dream was real. Sometimes, if Ellie closed her eyes tight, she could feel the touch of Mama's trunk and see her heart- shaped tusks. For a moment, the tears would subside until Ollie's cries grew louder. Ellie wrapped her trunk around her brother the way Mama used to do when he had a bad dream. When Ollie's whimpers fell to a whisper, Ellie would finally cry herself to sleep.

Welcome to the Sanctuary

Nerdi always wanted to visit the Savanna, but she wished it were under better circumstances. She was also glad that Mama could come with her to help. The flight was so long and Nerdi worried the whole time about her friend and his friends that she barely slept. During the ride to the Sanctuary, she rested her head in Mama's lap and tried to nap, unsure of what she could do to help. If her friend needed her, then she had to come. Mama was getting filled in on all the details by their driver, Nyela, one of the gazelle guard caretakers at the Sanctuary.

"Ashura has told us that your little one is very smart and very brave. She made quite an impression on him," Nyela said to Mama as she held her helpful and napping Nerdi in her arms. "Thank you both for coming here to help us."

"Nerdine loves her friends," Mama smiled, fluffing Nerdi's puffs. "Her and Ashura became close when he was in Cottontail Burrow. He was always at our house for muffins and buttery jam."

"Buttery jam?" Nyela asked.

"Yes, it is one of Nerdi's favorite things to eat. Perhaps, if I can find the ingredients or similar ones here, I will make some for everyone."

"That would be very nice," Nyela replied. "We need a bit of cheer since Ollie and Ellie have arrived. Now that you and Nerdine are here, I have hope that things will get better. Those poor elephants need a bit of cheer and good news. We found Ollie and Ellie a few miles from the main gate, exhausted from running all the way here."

"How did they know to come to the Sanctuary?" Mama asked.

"Elephants have amazing memory. Ollie and Ellie's aunt and mother were raised here. When Tussie—that's their mother—had babies of her own, she would bring them back to visit all the time. Eventually they became good friends with my Ashura."

"Your Ashura?" Mama asked.

"Our guard takes care of the orphans that show up here or that we find on patrols," Nyela explained. "On my first patrol, I found Ashura wandering around all alone. He became the first orphan under my care and has become like a son to me. So yes, he is my Ashura."

"You certainly did a wonderful job raising him."

"He spoke highly of you and Nerdi in his letters and calls home. So, I am not surprised that he called you to come help."

"Well, we just hope that we can help with whatever you need," Mama said as she stroked Nerdi's fur and took in the beautiful landscape of the Savanna.

When the truck came to a stop, Mama whispered, "Nerdine...Nerdine..." Nerdi whimpered softly and slowly fluttered open her eyes. "We are here," Mama said. Nerdi sat up, stretching her arms and legs while rolling her head a few times to loosen her neck. Looking around the sanctuary, there were little rhinos and giraffes and elephants each with gazelle caretakers.

Nerdi felt some sadness seeing so many young without mamas. Yet seeing each gazelle care for them and love them gave Nerdi hope. She held on to Mama's paw for a moment; grateful that she was here with her to help, but even more grateful that her mama would be here with her for whatever was to come.

"Nerdi!" yelled a familiar voice. Ashura smiled as he ran to his friend. "It is so good to see you and your mama, again! Thank you for coming. I'll take you in to meet Ollie and Ellie once you get settled in your quarters." Mama and Nerdi followed Nyela to the guest house. After placing their things in their room, Nerdi and Mama went back out to meet Ashura. They were eager to be introduced to Ollie and Ellie, who were staying in the quarters next door.

Ashura opened the door to the room slowly. "Ellie?" Ashura whispered to the elephant sitting by a window. "I told you she would come. These are my friends from Cottontail Burrow. They're here to help." Ellie looked over at Nerdi and Mama, her eyes heavy and swollen with tears.

"Help us?" Ellie asked, "How can anyone from so far away help us?"

"Nerdine is the smartest bunny I know," Ashura assured her, "If anyone can help us find your herd, she can!"

Nerdi walked over to Ellie, past the bed where Nyela stroked a sleeping Ollie's side. She started to put her paw out for Ellie to shake, but that didn't feel like enough. Instead, she embraced Ellie and Mama hugged them both. The little elephant, heavy with sorrow, melted into the hug, and for a moment Ellie's grief was eased.

"We are so sorry, Ellie," Mama said and started to pull away, but Ellie held on a bit longer.

"Do you think they're still out there?" Ellie asked. "Do you think you can find them?"

Nerdi would usually say that nothing was ever 100 percent, and she knew this was one of those times where it might be way less than 100 percent. The Savanna was massive, and she had no idea where to begin her search, but she couldn't say that. This was one of those times where it *had* to be 100 percent. Nerdi could not fail.

Looking at a tearful Ellie rest her head against the windowpane, Nerdi too wanted to cry. Her paw was balled into a tight fist and her face felt unusually warm, but with a heat that wasn't coming from the sun. For the first time, Nerdi didn't know what to say.

What could she say to make the grieving

elephant in front of her, who had lost so much, feel better? There was nothing she could say. She had to *do* something.

Stumped for Solutions

Nyela was able to get Ollie back asleep and came over to join Nerdi by the window. "We want to find Ollie and Ellie's herd," Nyela began, "but we also want to stop poachers from taking elephant tusks and rhino horns. All of the babies you see here are here because poachers leave them without a mother to care for them." Nerdi nodded in silent understanding.

"Ellie," Nerdi began, "I don't want you to tell me all of what happened, but is there anything you remember that can help us find who did this? Ashura mentioned that you saw the poacher that was after your mom. What do you remember?"

Ellie paused and retold Nerdi what she saw and heard. Nerdi listened carefully and something in the details sounded strangely familiar. Ellie finished, "It was dark, just moonlight, and I wish I paid closer attention. But I do remember his voice—I'll never forget his voice—how he sounded so sure that he was doing the right thing, even though it was wrong. He also had a long face with short stubby claws."

Nerdi exchanged a knowing glance with Mama and her whiskers began to twitch. "I have one more question about the voice you heard, Ellie. Did it start bragging about being the best, or that they knew more than the other poachers they were with?"

Ellie thought for a moment and said, "Yes, I did hear that. He said he knew more than anyone about tusks."

"I think I know who you saw that night," Nerdi announced.

Ellie thought for a moment and said, "

"Already?" questioned Nyela and Ashura.
Nerdi nodded and said, "His name is Gator Stump."

"We don't have gators in the Savanna," said Nyela, "Crocodiles for certain, but no gators. Are you sure?"

"Well," Ashura began, "Nothing is ever 100 percent, right Nerdi?"

Nerdi smiled at her friend, tickled that he remembered her mantra. "Usually, I'd say nothing is ever 100 percent, but trust me—I'm 100 percent sure that this gator gets around."

Nerdi went outside to think. Gator Stump. *Gator Stump*. Nerdi thought that problem floated away in the bayou the last time they met. It turns out the problem just went somewhere else to cause new problems for someone else. Nerdi's whiskers began to twitch, but not in the way she was used to them twitching.

She had quite a few things that needed figuring out. Where was Ollie and Ellie's herd? Were they alright? Where would she even start to look for them and could she find them like she promised? How would she stop Gator Stump and other poachers from taking more tusks? She didn't want any other elephants to go through what Ollie and Ellie did—so how do you stop Stump from stealing more tusks? Why did he want tusks anyway?

Nerdi pulled out her Paw Pad to do some research when Mama came out to talk to her.

"Are you alright, Nerdine?" Mama asked.

"No, Mama, I'm not okay. This is horrible what happened to Ollie and Ellie. I *have* to help them, but I don't know where to start. I need to find their herd and I need to stop Stump from hurting anyone else!"

"Well, Stump is taking tusks—do we know why? What's so special about them?" Mama gently interrogated.

"I don't know," Nerdi replied, "but a lot of these orphans are here because their parents were victims of poachers. How do we find Ollie and Ellie's herd *and* find a way to protect elephant tusks and rhino horns?"

"Remember when you were a little bunny and I wanted you to stop eating all of the tomatoes?"

"Yes, you only put out yellow and green ones. I wouldn't touch them because they weren't red." Nerdi said.

"Right, so why don't you figure out a way to do *that* for the elephants?"

Nerdi thought hard about what Mama was saying— she was sure this wasn't about tomatoes—then her whiskers began to twitch. Twitch in the way she liked.

"You're a genius, Mama! "Nerdi exclaimed. "Tusks are made of ivory. Ivory is white. Maybe if we change the color of the tusks, the poachers won't want the ivory. It has to be a color that can't be removed but also doesn't hurt the elephants. Maybe that could work! Even on the rhinos!"

"I knew you'd come up with something," Mama said, "You always do. I'm going to stick around here and help take care of Ollie and Ellie. They could use a mama's touch right now. Is that okay?"

"Of course, Mama. I'm glade you're here. Ollie and Ellie could use the help."

Nerdi went back to her room to pack her backpack. Soon it would be time for her to head out with Ashura and Nyela to search for Ollie and Ellie's herd. Finding the herd was important, but so was stopping poachers from taking tusks and horns.

Mama had the right idea of making them unappealing—but it had to stick and not be harmful to the rhinos and elephants. Nerdi had a feeling she would find the answer on her journey, and with a kiss and a hug from Mama, off she went.

Rhino Problems, Mane Events

The trek through the Savanna was brutal at times. They were lucky to have a truck with a canopy to protect them from the heat of the African sun. As they drove down the road, Nerdi took in every bush, watering hole and tree where she noticed spotted cats hiding.

"Are those…leopards?" Nerdi asked.

"Yes, napping no doubt after a long night of hunting," Ashura answered.

"Where are we headed, first?" Nerdi asked.

"Rhino Town. We'll stock up on supplies and camp there tonight," Nyela said.

Rhino Town was a bustling village full of bright colors and activity and shops. Nerdi noticed right away that many of the rhinos did not have horns, which she thought was peculiar.

"We can get our shopping done faster if we split the list, Ashura. You and Nerdi can get our food and water. I'll take care of the rest." Ashura nodded and off they went, dipping in and out of the shops, wading through the wares for sale. There were so many spices, fruits and nuts that Nerdi had never seen before, and the fragrant air from the different things was delicious. Ashura and Nerdi made sure to check off all the items on the list.

Nerdi also gathered a few extra souvenirs for Mama and the twins. As they finished their shopping and met up with Nyela, the elder of the village greeted Nerdi and her companions.

"Welcome to Rhino Town! I see you have purchased provisions. We have a space for you to make camp and rest before continuing on your journey."

"Thank you, Vifaru," said Nyela. "This is Nerdine, the friend of Ashura I was telling you about. She is visiting us to help find Ollie and Ellie's herd."

"Ahh, yes. Welcome to the Savanna, Nerdine. I wish it were under more celebratory circumstances," said Vifaru.

"Me too," Nerdi answered, "but I'm still finding ways to take in the beauty of the Savanna. Do you mind if I ask you a question, sir?"

"Of course," Vifaru leaned in.

"Why don't some of the rhinos here have horns?" Nerdi asked.

"We remove our horns to protect us from the poachers. This does not always work. Sometimes a poacher can see that a rhino doesn't have a full horn but will hunt us for it anyway. We have had several members of our tribe disappear. When we find what's left of the missing rhino, it is always the same: what remains of their horn is always gone. It is a terrible injustice."

"When you remove the horn, does it hurt?" Ashura asked.

"No," replied Vifaru, "but it is uncomfortable. Our horns are like your nails. If you don't cut down too far, it will not hurt. The horns grow back in about a year and if a rhino chooses, they will have it cut again."

"You still have your horns. Aren't you afraid that you'll be taken, too?" Nerdi asked.

"I keep my horns to protect the other rhinos. It is a risk, but a necessary one; one that Tussie understood. I am glad her little ones made it to the Sanctuary. How are they holding up?"

"Ellie is trying to be strong for her brother, but they're both struggling," said Nyela. "We need to find the rest of their herd. Do you have any idea where it could have gone?"

"No," Vifaru replied. "Given what happened to them, it is possible that they have scattered across the Savanna. One of our lookouts said he saw an elephant wandering a week ago, also looking for members of his herd. If you are able to talk to the lions tomorrow, they may have clues to offer. The lions tend to know everything."

"Then that's where we will start," Nerdi said, determined. "We will head there in the morning."

Nerdi and her companions thanked Vifaru for his help and set up camp. Exhausted from the journey, they fell asleep after dinner.

At night, the Savanna doesn't sleep; between bits of stillness and rustling grasses is the sound of a distant rumbling or roar. Nyela and Ashura didn't wake up at all, but these sounds were new to Nerdi. As tired as she was, she still slept with one eye open through the night. It was the quiet that woke her, just in time to see the sunrise. Nerdi breathed in the color and light. The sun rose, wrapped in a faded sky of purple, pink and blue.

"It's beautiful, isn't it," Nyela whispered.

"I never knew you could see all those colors in the sky at once," Nerdi softly replied.

"Sunrise in the Savanna feels like renewed purpose— and we have that today," Nyela said as she woke up Ashura. The three travelers packed up their camp and thanked the rhinos again for their hospitality. Then they set off on a two-day journey to meet the lions.

When Nerdi, Nyela and Ashura arrived, they could hear music before they made it through the clearing. Kiburi Mlima was a thriving community of lions and lionesses.

To Nerdi's right and to her left, there were manes of every color and texture. Some purple and silky, others yellow and bushy and some blue and curly. "Do all the lions here have manes? I've never seen lions like this before," Nerdi said in amazement, not thinking that anyone was listening.

"And you probably won't, not for miles," shouted a voice from behind her. "You're not from around here—I can tell. My name is Jibari. What brings you to Kiburi Mlima?"

"We're out looking for a group of elephants-" Ashura began.

"Ahh, that herd that got separated?" Jibari interjected.

"Yes," Ashura continued, "Have you—"

"Terrible!" Jibari interrupted again, "Awful. And yes, we know all about it. Everyone has been on high alert around here for any suspicious characters." Jibari paused and examined each of the visitors carefully. "You three look like suspicious characters..."

"Suspicious?" said another lion walking past, "Please stop picking on that bunny and her friends. One of them is Nyela—you know her!"

Jibari looked at Nyela again. "Ohhhh! It is Nyela. How have you been? She looks different today."

"Forgive my friend and his terrible manners. My name is Mtemi, the one in charge around here. You can call me Temi for short. Follow me."

Nerdi looked around at the lively community of lions. "It's beautiful here. Color everywhere..."

"I'd like to think most things are more beautiful on the mountain," Mtemi said. "We can see everything from here."

"So, you know what happened to that herd of elephants a while ago?" Nyela asked.

"Yes, as Jibari was saying, terrible tragedy," Mtemi's voice trailed off as the lion put their paw over their heart, "...and then how they all got separated..."

"Do you maybe know where they could be or point us in the right direction? We just came from the rhinos and they seemed to think you could help us," Ashura questioned.

"It's a shame they are cutting off their horns to protect them from poachers. Rhinos need their horns like elephants need their herds,"Mtemi said.

"Do you think we could do something like that to help the elephants?" Nerdi asked.

"Oh no. That won't work at all. Tusks are much different than horns. They don't grow back if you cut them. Tusks are like two teeth for the elephants, so when these poachers take an elephant's tusks, well…" Mtemi's voice trailed off again.

"How do you get your manes in all the colors? Do the lionesses have manes too?" Nerdi asked.

"Here, any lion can wear a mane--lion or lioness—it doesn't matter. We do things a bit differently than other lions in the Savanna. For example, I am a lioness, who happens to wear a mane. Jibari, who you met earlier, is a lion and he does not. That group of lions over there wear manes but with color. Here you get to be your true and best self—in whatever color, shade, mane or no mane."

Nerdi thought about the talk she had with Mama before leaving the sanctuary. "How do you color your manes? Could you come back with us to the Sanctuary and show them your process? I think if we were able to make the tusks different colors it would stop the poachers from wanting them."

"That's an idea, little bunny," Mtemi agreed. "Tell you what, I will go there with some lions to color the tusks of a few elephants and see how it goes."

"Wonderful! Can you leave right now?" Nyela asked.

"I suppose after The Prowl," Mtemi replied.

"What is The Prowl?" Ashura asked.

"It is a competition we have here to see which lion has the best stalk."

Nerdi and Ashura exchanged confused looks. Nyela simply smiled.

"Don't all lions stalk the same?" asked Nerdi.

Mtemi raised an eyebrow and laughed.

"Maybe where you come from. Come! Come! You'll see."

Pride. Stalk. Prowl.

Nerdi, Nyela, and Ashura made their way through the crowd with their lion escort. Nerdi looked around and saw that many of the lions were in groups dressed in an assortment of colorful and fun costumes.

"Leos, Lions, and Lionesses--let's get this started," bellowed a voice above the purrs and roars.

"Who is that?" Ashura asked.

"That's the announcer for The Prowls," Mtemi said, "Watch."

"Welcome to The Prowl!" At once all the lions began to roar and cheer. The announcer continued, "We had some fantastic stalking last week, but this afternoon is going to be a challenge. The first category is...*You've got to be kitten me.* I want to see your best stalk as cute kitten cubs. Do we have a volunteer to be the judge and prey today?"

"Right here!" Mtemi yelled pushing Nerdi through the crowd. "We have a visitor!"

"Oh, no Temi. I couldn't possibly—" Nerdi said as she tried to make her way back into the crowd. "I don't know what to do!"

"No one is going to bite you, I promise," Mtemi said, "All you must do is judge the competitors on who does the best stalk as a kitten. When you're done, we can send someone to the Sanctuary, and you can continue your search."

Nerdi nervously pawed her paws as she made her way to the center. She could see Nyela and Ashura giving her the okay and cheering with the rest of the lions.

"Alright prowlers," shouted the announcer. "Stalk the bunny!!!"

Suddenly from the crowd came a very tall and slim lion, walking towards Nerdi. Before the lion reached her, it dropped on all fours and began to pounce and bounce back and forth like…a kitten! Nerdi smiled and began to giggle. Two smaller lions emerged and started to chase yarn. Another lion ran right up to Nerdi before falling on the ground and tapping Nerdi's feet.

"*Yasssssss!* Loving this playful kitten energy! How are you doing, little bunny?!"

Nerdi smiled and gave the announcer a few nods. Then the music started. The song was an extremely popular one, as all the lions began to sing along and behave like kittens in a display of color, pouncing, dancing, and joy.

> *You be you, and I'll be me.*
> *We can be whatever we want to be.*
> *Love is love and love is free!*
> *Just live your best life!!*

Nerdi had never seen anything like it, but she enjoyed it a lot and wished she could prowl, too. It was impossible to pick a winner because every lion did their best kitten impression. After thinking for a bit, Nerdi decided that the winners today were the "kittens" with the yarn.

After the prowling was over, the announcer named Radi, along with Mtemi, joined Nerdi and her friends for a chat.

"Have you been to the Sanctuary before, Radi?" Nerdi asked.

"Ha--," Radi laughed, "the Sanctuary?? Little bunny, they don't welcome lions like us at the Sanctuary."

"I don't think that's true," Ashura said, "I've seen lions there."

"You've seen regular lions. Not lions like us with our colorful manes. I don't think we would be welcome there."

Nerdi turned to Nyela, wondering why anyone would feel unwelcome at the Sanctuary and asked, "Everyone is welcome there, right Nyela?"

"Every lion here would be welcomed at the Sanctuary. It is a place for everyone that wants to call it home and those who don't otherwise have a home. I tell Radi this every time I see him."

Radi rolled his eyes and nodded at Nyela. "She's right. She does tell me this every time she sees me. It has been our experience that we are mostly unwelcome anywhere else except with our own, which is why Kiburi Mlima exists. To give lions and lionesses who are different the chance to be themselves without judgment or fear."

"Many of us were kicked out of our prides for being different," Mtemi explained, "but that never happens here. We've created our own family."

"My mama thinks that families are stronger when they stick together, and she said that family can be the one you were given and also the one you pick for yourself. I think this new family that you have created for yourselves is beautiful. There are two little elephants who lost their family and while I know the Sanctuary would be a great new one, we *must* find their original one. We could really use the help."

Radi exchanged looks with Mtemi and said, "Your mama is incredibly wise, little bunny. We're happy to help. I just want to caution you that tusks are a lot different than manes, so I don't know how well the color will stick. A few of us will head to the Sanctuary and you can continue your search for the herd. We saw a few of those poachers tracking them into the plains where the buffalo roam. That might be the next place for you to go."

Last Stop, Buffalo

Rain fell steady and warm as the three friends traveled to where the buffalo roamed, which was about a three-day journey, first by truck and then on foot. Before the friends became drenched to the bone, they took refuge inside a huge baobab tree to rest. Nyela lit a small fire to help them dry off and stay warm while waiting for the rain to subside. The company of friends were sleeping soundly when Nerdi heard a voice coming from outside.

"Who...is...in...there?" came a deep voice from outside of their tree. Not wishing to wake her companions, Nerdi peeked outside and saw a large buffalo staring remarkably close to her face.

"You...don't smell...like you're...from around here," the buffalo remarked.

"No," Nerdi whispered, "I'm an awfully long way from home. I'm here to help my friends find their family."

The buffalo replied, "Do you mean those elephants?"

"Yes, have you seen them?" asked Nerdi.

"I'm afraid I have not," the buffalo answered. "Actually, I don't see much of anything and I can't hear all that great either...but my herd did smell some elephants a few days back. You just missed them."

"Did you see—or smell—which way they went? We really need to find them," Nerdi replied.

"I did not. But if you follow me to the watering hole, maybe some of the other buffalo will be there and you can ask them."

Nerdi ducked back inside the tree and woke Nyela and Ashura. They grabbed their packs, exited the tree, and followed their new companion to the watering hole.

"You never told us your name," Ashura said as they walked across the plain.

The buffalo replied, "Oh, well you didn't introduce yourself to me either."

"That was rude of us. I am Ashura. The gazelle is Nyela and the bunny you met is Nerdine—she's come all the way across the ocean from a place called Cottontail Burrow to help us find the elephants."

"Oh my," said the buffalo, "Do you always journey so far to help find families that you don't know?"

"I would travel anywhere to help a friend," Nerdi smiled. "Ashura is my friend. I hope we can become friends, too. But it would help if you told us *your* name."

"Oh yes," the buffalo replied with a slow deep chuckle, "Mbogo. My name is Mbogo. I would like us to be friends very much."

"Whoa…" Nerdi gasped as they came through a clearing of grass, "This is your herd?"

"Yes," Mbogo answered. "We are many and that makes us mighty even though no one thinks of us that way."

"Who is that with you, Mbogo?" a buffalo, bellowed from the crowd.

"It's okay, Nyati. Everyone—these are new friends. They have come here looking for old friends."

"I'm sure it isn't us," Nyati began, "no one really talks to us or pays attention to us. We're outsiders I suppose. Too fat, too blind, and too deaf for anyone to really care about us. So, we have to take care of each other—and stay close. That's how we stay safe you know—by sticking together."

"Your herd is magnificent. I am so happy to have met you. Pardon my manners, I'm Nerdi. I'm here to help my friends find a group of elephants that may have come this way."

"Your old friends were here," Nyati responded. "Some strangers came around stalking those elephants. One of them even tried to take one of our herd—but we scared him off and chased him away."

"Yes," said Mbogo, "We might seem slow and fat, but we can be fast!"

"We've lost a few over the years unfortunately. Not without a fight though," Nyati continued.

"Everything happened so quickly that once the dust settled, we lost track of the elephants. Sorry we don't have more information for you. Bad eyes and ears, you know."

"Thank you for your help." Nerdi sat on the ground, put her face in her paws and groaned. Ashura sat next to his friend and gently rubbed her back.

"We've been out here for over a week, Nerdi," Nyela said as she sat next to Nerdi on the ground. "We really need to head back to the Sanctuary." She turned to Mbogo and Nyati. "Thank you for your help, and you are always welcome to bring the herd to the Sanctuary."

"Dangerous times we are in," Mbogo replied. "We may take you up on that, but we have to decide that as a group you know."

"I understand," Nyela responded.

Nerdi, Ashura and Nyela returned to their camp in the baobab tree, gathered their things, and walked back to their truck. With the heaviest of hearts, they piled inside and began their long journey home.

No Bunny is 100 Percent

When Nerdi and her companions made it back to the preserve, they noticed many more residents were there than when they left over a week ago. As Nerdi gathered her pack from the truck, a member of the Gazelle Guard ran up to Nyela to give her a report of what had happened since they left.

"Welcome back. I'm glad you have returned safely. The lions from Kiburi Mlima arrived and have been hard at work attempting their coloring techniques on the rhinos and elephants here at the Sanctuary. On the way here, they heard that the elephants we're looking for are somewhere in the grasslands on the other side of the Sanctuary near the buffalo."

"Where we just came from? We were so close! We have to go back and see if they're there!" Nerdi whimpered. She was determined to complete the mission she gave herself, but Nyela looked at the bunny's dry fur, disheveled puffs, and heavy eyes, and she could see that Nerdi was in no condition to travel.

"No, Nerdine. This time you have to stay put," Nyela said.

"But—" Nerdi began to argue, but Nyela shut her down immediately.

"No buts! I promised your mother that I would take care of you. You just got back, and you need to rest for a few days. I will send a fresh search party in the morning to see if they can find any sign of Ollie and Ellie's herd. I promise. But I need you to go rest or see if Mama needs help. Please."

Jibari and Mtemi emerged from a tent, covered mane to paw in shades of pink, blue, and lavender.

"None of these will take," Jibari exclaimed, "They was right out!"

"We have tried, pink, purple, blue, orange, red, yellow—none of it will stick to the tusks or the horns. I simply cannot understand it," said Mtemi.

Coloring tusks and horns was the best idea Nerdi had and now it was a failed idea. Worst still, it was a failed idea that gave the rhinos and elephants hope, which Nerdi thought was worse than not having an idea at all. She was also no closer to finding Ollie and Ellie's herd. Never had there been a problem that Nerdi couldn't think her way through. As she wracked her brain for the next idea, she looked around and saw just how many arrivals had come to the Sanctuary because their parents were missing.

Nerdi headed over to visit Ollie when one of the caretakers came out of his room with a tray of food.

"Is Ollie alright?" asked Nerdi.

The caretaker looked down and shook her head.

"Ollie has stopped eating and refuses to leave his bed. If he doesn't eat…"

Nerdi's heart sank into her stomach. By this point, she would have another idea, say something about nothing ever being 100 percent and then have things figured out. The way things were going right now, Nerdi would take 25 percent of a so-so idea. She knew she needed to deal with the poachers, but the Savanna was enormous—the lion and rhino communities were spread out in the enormousness. There was just too much space to cover for one little bunny and the Gazelle Guard. As Nerdi felt completely overwhelmed, Mama came out to sit with her.

"Mama…I don't think I can fix this," Nerdi whispered—exhausted with tears in her eyes.

Mama placed her soft, warm arms around her little girl and asked, "Who asked you to fix it, Nerdine?"

"That's what I do, Mama. Ashura asked me to come here to stop the elephants from getting hurt. Every day there's a new elephant or rhino here because…because I failed!" Nerdi wiped the tears flowing slowly down her face. "They keep getting hurt because I can't fix it! On top of that, I can't find Ollie and Ellie's family—if they still have a family—and Gator Stump is still out there…"

"Whoa, Nerdine! You put too much on yourself," Mama said as she comforted and hugged her daughter, who now sobbed deeply in her arms.

"Ashura asked you for help to find Ollie and Ellie's family. I know you want to stop Stump from separating elephants from their herds, but you can't do everything on your own. It's not fair to expect that of yourself. All you can do is your best, hope that others will pitch in with their best, and together you leave things better than you found them."

Mama rocked Nerdi in her arms, each soft sway subsiding Nerdi's tears. Ollie stood in the door watching and thinking that if his mama were here, she would say the same things.

"Nerdine?" Ollie whispered weakly as he sat next to her. Nerdi turned to face him. "I hope you find our herd. But if you don't, I'm glad you were here, and you tried."

Mama hugged the little elephant and Nerdi. Ollie wasn't sure that things were going to be alright. He realized that he may never see his herd again, but for that moment, he was glad to be with someone who made him and his sister feel loved; that they weren't forgotten and they certainly were not alone.

Showdown at the Falls

Nyela said Nerdi needed to rest for a few days, but rest only gave Nerdi time to think about everything going wrong. She tried to spend her time playing games with Ollie and Ellie or telling them stories of her other adventures—anything to distract them and keep their spirits up. Mama made buttery jam using some of the ingredients from the market in Rhino Town. Upon tasting it for the first time, Ollie and Ellie smiled in a way that no one had seen them smile since they arrived. At night, Nerdi noticed that it's never really quiet at the Sanctuary. The sound of life fighting on in spite of circumstance was the soundtrack that surrounded you as part of the air. Nerdi couldn't sleep most nights anyway, so naturally on the third night, she could hear the commotion outside.

Throwing on her clothes, Nerdi ran to see what was happening. There were lions, rhinos, buffalo, leopards and bees outside of the gates. Ashura was there trying to gain information.

"What's going on, Ashura?" Nerdi asked.

"I think they are here to help," Ashura answered. "It looks like word got around to the entire Savanna about Ollie and Ellie's herd."

Nerdi recognized the buffalo that spoke next; it was Mbogo. "You made a very strong impression after you left."

Then Vifaru spoke. "It's not just on you to help us, Nerdi, but on all of us. The gazelles have been doing their best for a long time, but now we have to help, too."

Radi from Kiburi Mlima also spoke. "You were right. We can't just stay on the sidelines or among our own. We are all in this fight. As you said, we are stronger together. Today, it's the elephants. Next, it could be the lions or giraffes. We need to work together to keep us *all* safe. So how do we find this gator named Stump and get him OUT of our Savanna?"

The pause felt like hours. In her mind Nerdi wrestled with joy, sadness, and relief. There were so many things that she wanted to say, but all that mattered was Ollie and Ellie. Taking a deep breath, Nerdi finally answered, "I don't know. He's probably trying to find the rest of Ollie and Ellie's herd to take their tusks. We can't let happen."

"We sent out a search party this morning to look in the grasslands but have not heard anything yet," Nyela reported.

A leopard came forward and said, "We spotted an outsider in the grasslands today. If he and his group are out there tracking the elephants, they might still be there. We can cover more ground if we are all searching."

"I agree," said Nyela. "The sun comes up in a few hours. I say we head out then. With more eyes and ears, we can find these poachers and maybe the herd before anyone else gets hurt."

Nerdi nodded. Then, for the remaining twilight, she and the volunteers gathered supplies. She began to feel better and a bit more hopeful. Maybe Mama was right about pitching in and with so many here they had to give it their best. At first light, they set out into the grasslands.

The search party was broken up into three groups: Group 1 stayed close to the perimeter of the Sanctuary. Group 2 headed northeast. Group 3 went northwest. Each group had a small swarm of bees to provide information from the air and report over the radio.

"No sign of the herd in the northwest corner or near the perimeter," buzzed the swarm.

Soon came exciting news. "We have movement in the Northwest," the bees buzzed. "A small party of poachers. Looks like they have found something...could be the herd. All groups should make their way to the Northwest Falls. Protect the herd!"

"Do you have a positive identification on the gator?" asked Ashura.

There was a pause before a voice buzzed back over the radio, "Yes, we can confirm it is the gator called Stump near the falls."

Everyone stampeded as fast as their limbs would carry them to the Northwest Falls. The lions and rhinos surrounded the poachers on the right, while the gazelles and leopards shielded the elephants on the left. The buffalo mobbed the poachers down the middle, scaring them off; thus, giving the elephants a chance to turn and run. Stump, now alone, came face to face with a familiar foe.

"How could you do that to Ollie and Ellie's mama?!" Nerdi shouted.

Stump looked at Nerdi with a clueless expression followed by a sinister cackle.

"Who? What's an Ollie and Ellie?" Stump sneered before pausing a few seconds and continuing, "Ohhh, are those the baby elephants? What do you want from me? I let them go. Not enough tusk on them yet for me. That big one though—she was magnificent. Most beautiful tusks I've ever seen; and they'll look great on my wall!" Stump chortled as he turned his back towards the bunny.

Nerdi felt heat rise in her cheeks. Her vision blurred such that she could only focus on Stump but heard Ashura's news on the radio and she knew what she had to do. Her paws clinched into tiny fists as she screamed and bounded as fast as she could towards Stump!

The gator turned back around and began to laugh loudly saying, "Ha! Are you coming to fight me tiny bunny? You're adorable! Bring it on!" Stump charged snarling violently at Nerdi. Just as he was about to reach her, a swarm of bees flew in front of him, blocking his view of the young bunny!

"What are you doing?!" Stump snapped as he went into a flurry of floundering and swatting. "Get out of my way! If the bunny is feeling brave, let her come! I'll even give her the first punch!" More and more bees surrounded Stump as he continued to snarl and swat; swatting so much that he forgot how

close he was to the edge of the falls and fell right
over the top!

As the dust settled and the bees dispersed, the group realized that they had won, saving the elephants from the poachers. But as the victors looked around, they noticed that Nerdi, Ashura and Nyela were nowhere to be found!

Forever Family

It was a bittersweet victory as the search group headed back to the Sanctuary. Stump was gone and so were the poachers, but the herd ran off again. This time no one saw which way they went. To make matters even worse, Nerdi, Nyela, and Ashura were now missing.

"No one saw where they went?" asked Radi.

"No, we lost sight of them. Everything was happening so fast!" yelled the bees.

At that moment, four elephants approached the outside gate. Ollie was sitting with his sister on a tuft of grass under a tree when he looked up and saw them.

"Aunt Izzie?" Ollie cried with half hope and half disbelief. "Ellie...look! Is that Aunt Izzie?" His sister sat up to look towards the gate. Her eyes widened and her mouth opened with a gasping smile. The siblings were on their feet, walking and half-running to the gate. As they got closer, their eyes filled with tears, but their mouths let out trumpets of joy that no one had heard from them since they arrived. The herd found *them*. What's more, Nerdi, Ashura and Nyela were with them!

"You found them!" Ollie cried. "You said you would find them, and you did!"

Turns out, Ashura was watching as the herd took off and saw which way they were headed. After the bees got between Nerdi and Stump, Ashura, Nerdi and Nyela ran as fast as their feet could carry them to catch up to the herd and bring them back to the Sanctuary.

"We didn't think it was safe to come here," Izzie said. "The poachers were everywhere. I was trying to find everyone after that night. If we weren't hiding, we were running. We wanted to come here first. This is where Tussie and I grew up and I knew she would send her children here, but the poachers tracked us everywhere. I was trying to keep the herd together and safe. I'm sorry it took so long to get here."

"It would have taken longer, if not for these brave ones," Nyela said.

Shaking her head, Nerdi said, "I can't take any credit for this. Ashura was able to see where you were going. If not for him, we would have lost you again."

Ashura now shaking his head, "No, Nerdine— don't be so modest. You were a warrior out there today facing Stump."

"Then three trumpets for Ashura *and* Nerdi!" Izzie shouted. Ollie, Ellie, and all the elephants let out three victorious trumpets in thanks for what the two friends had done.

"Please, Izzie—stay here with us," Nyela pleaded with the elephant. "The Sanctuary has more than enough room, and we can look after you."

"I think that's a good idea," said Ellie.

"I don't ever want to be separated from you again," Ollie chimed in as he and Ellie hugged their aunt.

Nerdi was relieved. It turns out, 25 percent of a *so-so* plan is sometimes all you need. "Stump might be gone," Nerdi said, "but more poachers may come."

"Nerdine is right," said Nyela speaking to everyone that could hear, "We are a family here and we must care for each other. *Our* sanctuary must grow and be a home for all."

"We should rename it, Nyela," Ashura said. "How about...Nyumba? Since this is home for every lion, elephant, buffalo, rhino, leopard--anyone that wants one. All are welcome here."

Nyela smiled with pride at her sweet Ashura. "That is perfect. Any of you that wishes to stay is welcome to do so. We have plenty of room!" Nyela turned her attention to Nerdi. "You as well, *Shujaa* Bunny."

"*Shujaa?*" Nerdi asked. "What does it mean?"

"It means, *Warrior*," replied Nyela. "You are the bravest bunny I have ever met, Nerdi. You and Mama will always have a second home here."

Nyela and Nerdi hugged. Nerdi whispered softly, "Thank, you." When they let go of their embrace, Nyela gave Nerdi a salute, and each member of the Gazelle Guard followed, saluting in unison.

After a few more days, Nerdi and Mama bid their new friends farewell and returned to their home in Cottontail Burrow to some *extremely disappointed* twins.

"WAIT!" You and Mama spent the WHOLE summer on SAFARI?! Are you kidding me right now?" Sporty grumbled.

"Lions and rhino and leopards, oh my!" chuckled Artsy as he stuffed a piece of muffin in his mouth.

"To be fair, Sporty, it's not like it was a relaxing vacation. Nerdi was--"

"I know, Mama," Sporty interrupted, " She was down there to help." Sporty refocused her attention on her big sister. "We are *not* going to camp next year. Every summer you go do something cool while we're away at camp painting pottery and making s'mores!"

"Wait a minute," Artsy grumbled, muffin crumbs falling out his mouth, "What's wrong with s'mores?!"

"Nothing," continued Sporty, "but these adventures we keep missing? This is starting to get ridiculous. If Nerdi goes to the North Pole next summer, Artsy and I are going with her!" Sporty huffed, nodded, and bounced to her room.

A few days before school started, photos and a letter arrived from the Nyumba Sanctuary.

Dear Nerdi and Mama:

Ollie and Ellie are doing much better now that their herd is here. They have decided to stay with us at Nyumba for now. We scared away the rest of the poachers, but some still come.

Sometimes we get new orphans, but with all of us working together, it is a lot less than it has been in a long time.

I know you don't want to take the credit for reuniting Ollie and Ellie, but it was you that said we should run after them once Stump was distracted. If we would have waited, we may have lost them again. So, thank you, my friend. I hope you have a wonderful school year, Shujaa.

Your friend always,
Ashura

P.S. Even though it is temporary, the lions will dye whatever you want: tusks, horns, manes, hooves—you name it! As you can see from the photos, we are all one colorful family!

Nerdi Notes

- *Elephants, lions, rhino, leopards, and buffalo represent the "Big 5" of Africa's savanna.*

- *Elephants and rhinos are in constant danger due to poaching and trophy hunting for their tusks and horns.*

- *Ollie and Ellie's mama, Tussie is a tusker elephant. Tuskers have exceptionally long tusks that grow long enough to touch the ground. As of 2019, there are less than 30 left in the world.*

- *The character names and places are in Kiswahili. This is the official language of at least five African countries, including Kenya and Tanzania—the inspiration for the setting of the Savanna in the story.*

- *Nyela and the Gazelle Guard are based on the Akashinga, an all-female anti-poaching unit based in Zimbabwe.*

- There are several wonderful organizations that help protect these beautiful animals. Please visit their sites to learn more about what they do and how you can help:

- Sheldrick Wildlife Trust
- Tsavo Trust
- International Anti-Poaching Foundation
- Reteti Elephant Sanctuary
- Kenya Wildlife Trust

Thank you for reading Nerdi's third adventure!

Please leave us a review on Amazon and other book websites--then check out our other titles!

You can also connect with Nerdi Bunny and author Aisha Toombs on social media:

Twitter: @NerdiBunny &

@AishaToombs77 Instagram:

@nerdi.bunny &   @anicole1977

Or visit our website
www.NerdiBunny.com to keep up with all things #BrownBrainyBrilliant

Made in the USA
Middletown, DE
01 March 2022

61935449R00035